MELANIE BROWN CI

by the same author

Melanie Brown Goes To School

Melanie Brown
Climbs a Tree

Pamela Oldfield

Illustrated by
Carolyn Dinan

First published in 1972
by Faber and Faber Limited
3 Queen Square London WC1N 3AU
This paperback edition first published in 1989

Phototypeset by Input Typesetting Ltd, London
Printed and bound in Great Britain by
Richard Clay Ltd, Bungay, Suffolk

A CIP record for this book
is available from the British Library

ISBN 0-571-15465-4

Contents

*For Jonathan
and the children
of Ridgewell School*

Melanie Brown Climbs a Tree

Melanie Brown was nearly six years old and she went to the village school. She had a nice teacher whose name was Miss Bradley and they understood each other very well. She also had a great many friends but her favourite friend was a boy called Christopher. He was Melanie Brown's boy-friend, and they always walked home together after school.

One day Christopher had a bad cold and had to stay away from school, so when it was home time there was no one for Melanie Brown to walk with. She hated walking on her own, so she looked around for someone else to walk with. But no one was as nice as Christopher and she spent such a long time trying to make up her mind that suddenly there were only two boys left. They were Nigel and Dennis, two of the boys in the top class.

'I'll walk home with you,' she told them.

They looked at her in dismay.

'We don't walk home with girls!' said Nigel. 'They're soppy!'

'Girls are *not* soppy,' said Melanie Brown indignantly. 'And I'll have to walk with you because all the others have gone, and I don't like walking by myself.'

'Well, you can't walk with us,' said Nigel, 'because

we're not going home.'

'Not going home?' said Melanie Brown. 'Why aren't you going home?'

'Because we're going to do something else first, and it's a secret, so go away!'

But, of course, that made her all the more determined to stay. They shouted at her, and they pushed her away, but she took no notice.

'Tell me the secret, then,' she said, 'and I'll go away.'

They glared at her angrily, and then whispered together. At last Dennis said, 'We're going to climb a tree.'

Melanie Brown's eyes opened wide. She had never climbed a tree!

'I'll come with you,' she said, and nothing they could say or do could make her change her mind.

Behind the school kitchen was a big old oak tree. It was perfect for climbing because it had wide, spreading branches. Melanie Brown looked up into its green leaves and was quite delighted. She imagined how it would be to sit up there, hidden from view.

Dennis went up first. He went up quickly and easily, until suddenly his foot slipped. Melanie Brown gave a little scream.

'Shh!' warned Nigel. 'We're not supposed to be round here, so be quiet.'

She looked round anxiously.

'But there's no one to hear us,' she said.

'The teachers haven't gone home yet,' said Nigel.

Soon both the boys were up in the tree, looking down at Melanie Brown.

'If you don't help me up,' she said, 'I'll scream and scream and scream until someone hears me, and then I'll tell them you're up the tree!'

The boys muttered some very nasty things about girls but Dennis climbed down and helped her up. In no time at all she was sitting astride a wide branch, her head among the leaves. It was wonderful!

'It's just like a tree house,' she said breathlessly. 'Oh, let's play mothers and fathers!'

The boys looked at her without enthusiasm.

'This is our house,' she said, 'and I'm the mother, and you're the father and the uncle, and you have to go to work, while I make the dinner. These leaves can be the dinner – '

3

'We are *not* playing mothers and fathers,' said Nigel grimly, 'so shut up.'

Melanie Brown ignored him.

'That big branch can be the bedroom, and this is the kitchen and this is an upstairs flat because it's so high . . .'

Dennis and Nigel exchanged despairing looks, then quietly they began to climb down from the tree. She watched them go.

'That's right,' she said happily. 'You go to work, and when you come back the dinner will be ready.'

But the boys had had enough of Melanie Brown for one day. They climbed down from the tree, and they wandered off along the lane, and they did *not* come back. They left Melanie Brown in the tree all on her own!

Melanie Brown waited and waited for the father and the uncle to come home from work, but, of course, they never did. At first she was annoyed with them, then she began to get worried, and finally she got very frightened and tried to climb down but the tree was too high and she was too small. She began to wonder if she would be there all night, with the bats and the owls!

'Help me, someone,' she shouted. 'I'm up in the tree! Help me!'

There was no answer, so she shouted again and again, until at last she heard footsteps, and there was Mr Bloggs the caretaker, looking up at her in amazement.

'Blow me down!' he said. 'If it's not Melanie Brown!

4

I might have known it! Never met a girl like you for getting into mischief. I suppose I'll have to go and get my ladder.' And he went off to fetch it, grumbling to himself about 'young people today' not being what they were in his day.

When he came back Melanie Brown's mother was with him. She had come up to the school to look for Melanie Brown, when she did not come home from school. Mr Bloggs rested the ladder against the tree,

but still Melanie Brown was afraid to climb down. Mr Bloggs snorted. 'I suppose I'll have to carry you down,' he said. 'I'll give you a fireman's lift, that's what I'll do. Didn't know I used to be a fireman, did you?'

She agreed that she did not know. He went up the ladder and carried her safely down.

'I've got a photograph at home, of me in my fireman's uniform. I'll show it to you some time,' he said.

She said that she would like to see it. Then Mrs Brown thanked him for all his help, and they said 'goodbye' and hurried away down the lane. When they told Mr Brown what had happened he bought some tobacco for Mr Bloggs to smoke in his pipe. Melanie Brown gave it to him when she passed his cottage next morning, on her way to school. Mr Bloggs showed her the photograph, and she thought he looked very handsome in his uniform.

They have been good friends ever since.

Melanie Brown
and the Harvest Festival

Melanie Brown went home from school feeling very important. She had a note in her pocket which Miss Bradley had given her. She had kept it safely in her pocket all day without losing it. It was about the Harvest Festival. The headmistress had told them all about it.

'Autumn is harvest time,' she said. 'We want to thank God for all the good things he sends us. Fruit and vegetables and flowers. We say "thank you" by taking some of the things to church. Then, after the service, we give the things to old people who do not have much money.'

Melanie Brown thought it was a wonderful idea, and so did her mother.

'We'll ask Daddy if he can find you the two biggest apples on the tree,' she said, and of course, Daddy said he would. He took a ladder and climbed up into the branches of the apple tree. Melanie Brown held out her skirt, and he dropped the two biggest apples into it – one at a time, of course, so they did not bruise. She washed the apples under the tap and polished them with a soft cloth. They were big and green and shiny and she could hardly wait to show them to the other children.

She set off along the lane next morning carrying the apples very carefully. Soon Christopher joined her. He had a large cabbage tucked under his arm. His big blue eyes opened wide when he saw the big green apples.

'What giant apples!' he said.

She told him they were from her own tree.

'I wish I had an apple tree,' said Christopher wistfully. 'I love apples.'

Feeling suddenly generous Melanie Brown handed him one of the big green apples.

'You can have this one,' she said. 'I'm sure the old people won't mind.'

Christopher smiled one of his biggest smiles and took a large bite. Then he pulled an awful face.

'Sour!' he said briefly.

Melanie Brown took it back and handed him the other one to try. That was sour, too.

'They must be cooking apples,' he said. They

8

looked at the two big apples, each with a large bite out of it. Without a word Christopher tossed his over the hedge into the pond – splash. Melanie Brown's apple followed it with another splash!

'Now I haven't got anything for Harvest Festival,' said Melanie Brown, 'and it's all your fault!'

Before they could start to argue Denise ran up to them. She had a bundle of onions in a polythene bag. 'Aren't you bringing anything?' she asked Melanie Brown.

'Of course!' said Melanie Brown. 'I'm bringing mine tomorrow – so it will be nice and fresh.'

That evening she told her mother what had happened to the apples.

'You are a silly girl,' said her mother. 'Never mind. I'll find you something else for tomorrow, but it won't be apples because it's raining and I'm not going down the garden to get all wet.'

Next morning she gave Melanie Brown a small basket. Inside were a packet of biscuits, a jelly, and a big brown egg.

'That is all I can spare,' she said, 'so take care of it.'

Melanie Brown promised she would and set off for school once more. Half-way along the lane she realized that no one had joined her.

'I must be early,' she said to herself and decided to stop and have a closer look at the biscuits. There was a chocolate one and a wafer and one with icing on it and the more Melanie Brown looked at them the more she felt sure that the old people would not like them because they were too sweet. Melanie Brown's grandmother didn't like sweet biscuits and *she* was old!

'I'll just eat the sweet ones,' she told herself, 'and I'll leave the plain ones.'

It didn't seem quite right to stand in the lane eating the Harvest Festival biscuits, so she climbed over the gate into the field and sat down by the pond with her back against a tree. Now no one passing in the lane could see her. She opened the packet of biscuits and began to eat them. It was very pleasant by the pond with the sunlight glinting on the water. She could hear

voices in the lane and smiled to think how surprised the children would be if they could see her. When she had eaten all the biscuits she opened the jelly. It was in little squares, so she tasted a square and decided to eat that, too!

As she popped the last square into her mouth she suddenly noticed how quiet it was. There were no more voices in the lane. She jumped to her feet and the basket tumbled out of her lap. The big, brown egg rolled out and fell into the water, out of sight among the weeds.

'Well,' said Melanie Brown, 'that's that!'

She tossed the basket into a clump of stinging nettles and ran back to the gate. She ran along the lane to school and found the playground empty. The classroom was empty, too. She ran back into the lane and on to the church but before she reached the door the sound of music filled the air and she recognized the tune of 'All things bright and beautiful' which was her favourite hymn.

'They've started without me!' she told herself indignantly and hurried up to the door. She did mean to go in, but at the last moment her courage failed her. They might ask her about the biscuits and the jelly and the egg! Slowly she turned and made her way to a wooden seat by the path. She decided to wait for them instead and sat on the edge of the seat, swinging her legs.

'I wonder – ' she thought happily, 'I wonder what I'll bring for Harvest Festival next year!'

Melanie Brown's
First School Photograph

As soon as she heard the word 'photographer' Melanie Brown pricked up her ears. She didn't always pay a great deal of attention when Miss Bradley was talking to them, but this time she thought it sounded interesting.

'He won't be here until after dinner,' Miss Bradley told them, 'so try to keep yourselves clean and tidy.'

'Are we all going to be in the same photograph?' asked Paula.

'No,' said Miss Bradley. 'He will take a photograph of every child separately, except where there are brothers and sisters in the school. Then he will take a group.'

'But my sister's in the top class,' said Nicholas anxiously.

'It won't make any difference,' said Miss Bradley. 'We shall get all the children in each family together.'

Susan pulled a face.

'I don't want to be in a photograph with my brother,' she said. 'He's awful! I want to be on my own.'

'Well, you can't,' said Miss Bradley patiently. 'It would be too expensive for your mother and father to have to buy two photographs.'

'They're rich!' said Susan, but Miss Bradley only laughed and told them to remember what she had said about keeping clean.

Melanie Brown went straight into the cloakroom and looked at herself in the mirror. Her thick brown hair was tied in two bunches. She looked thoughtfully at the ribbons.

'Please may I go home?' she asked Miss Bradley. 'I want to get my best pink ribbons – they're pink velvet!'

'But, Melanie,' said Miss Bradley, 'whatever is wrong with those red ones you are wearing? They look very smart. Anyway, there is no time for you to go home. The dinner is almost ready. Hurry up and wash your hands.'

Melanie Brown picked up the soap and put it down again. She crossed to the mirror and looked at herself once more.

'I could take off the ribbons and wear my hair loose!' she said. 'Or I could have a pony tail – or two little plaits?'

Miss Bradley laughed.

'Melanie,' she said, 'you look very nice as you are. Your mother will want a photograph of you as you are at school. You can dress up and wear you hair differently when you have a photograph taken at home. Now do get a move on with that washing. We're all waiting for you.'

Melanie Brown was very displeased. She sat through dinner with a very grumpy face and wouldn't smile, not even when she saw that it was ginger pudding which was her favourite. Then, suddenly, she had another idea. As soon as the last plate was neatly stacked on the trolley she ran to find Christopher and tell him her idea. She found him sitting on the fence, so she climbed up beside him.

'Would you like to be in my photograph?' she asked him sweetly.

'Can't!' he said briefly.

'I'll ask Miss Bradley,' she urged, 'if you want to be in it.'

'But I'm not your brother,' said Christopher, 'and you're not my sister, so we aren't the same family – so we can't.'

'You are my best boy-friend,' said Melanie Brown, but Christopher said that Miss Bradley hadn't mentioned boy-friends.

'She forgot!' said Melanie Brown airily. 'I'll go and remind her.'

She found Miss Bradley cleaning the blackboard, and explained her idea.

'I'm sorry,' said Miss Bradley. 'A best boy-friend is not the same as family. Your mother wouldn't want a photograph with Christopher in it – and Christopher's mother won't want one with you in it! Do stop fussing and go out to play like a good girl.'

But Melanie Brown was *not* a good girl. She did not go out to play. She flew into a tantrum instead! She sobbed and wailed and argued and pleaded. She tossed her head and stamped her feet – she even shouted at Miss Bradley. But Miss Bradley just went on cleaning the blackboard and didn't take any notice at all. At

last Melanie Brown had to stop because she was worn out and tired of all the noise she was making, so she went into the Wendy House to recover.

Of course, when the photographer came she had her photograph taken without any fuss and she waited eagerly for the results. They came the next week in a big envelope. The photographs were in colour and each one was in a little white cardboard frame. The children were delighted – all except Melanie Brown.

The little girl in *her* cardboard frame looked very disagreeable and had red eyes from all that crying! Hastily she tucked the photograph into her satchel so that no one else should see how awful she looked. She had a nasty feeling that her mother and father were not going to be very pleased with her very first school photograph!

Melanie Brown and the Best Doll

Melanie Brown had a best doll. She had three dolls altogether – an old rag doll called Susie; a fairy doll who had lost her wand; and a baby doll called Sarah. Sarah was her best doll, because she had real golden hair, long eyelashes, and blue eyes that opened and shut. Grandmother knitted lots of pretty clothes for Sarah, and Melanie Brown was very proud of her.

One day she put Sarah's best dress on, and took her to school. When she went into the playground all the other girls crowded round to see the best doll.

'Isn't she lovely,' said Jennifer. 'May I hold her, please?'

'You can if you don't drop her,' said Melanie Brown, and she watched anxiously while Jennifer held Sarah. Then, of course, all the girls wanted to hold her, but the whistle blew and it was time to go into school.

Melanie Brown showed Sarah to Miss Bradley.

'Oh Melanie, what a lovely doll,' said Miss Bradley, 'and what a pretty dress she's wearing.'

'My Granny knitted it,' said Melanie Brown proudly.

'Your Granny must be very good at knitting.'

'She is.'

'Well, leave the doll here until we come out of prayers and then you can play with her.'

As soon as they were back in the classroom Melanie Brown took Sarah into the Wendy House and Denise, Paula and Christopher went in too. They played 'mothers and fathers' and it was great fun.

When it was time to do some writing Melanie Brown saw that the chair next to hers was empty because Pat was away from school. She asked Miss Bradley if Sarah could sit there and Miss Bradley said, 'Yes,' so the best doll sat next to her.

'I do hope Sarah won't talk too much,' said Miss Bradley, and that made all the children laugh.

At story-time Sarah sat on Melanie Brown's lap. It really was a very happy morning. At dinner-time, however, Denise went home and brought back *her* best doll. It was a 'walkie-talkie' doll called Catherine Elizabeth and all the girls began to admire Catherine Elizabeth instead of Sarah. Melanie Brown was not at all pleased.

'Catherine Elizabeth is very clever,' Denise told them. 'When I pull this cord she talks. Listen.'

She pulled a cord and the doll began to talk.

'What a silly, squeaky voice!' said Melanie Brown, but no one was listening to her. Then they all watched the doll walk.

'What a funny way to walk!' said Melanie Brown. 'She can't even bend her legs!'

Denise glared at her.

'Well, your doll can't even walk *or* talk, so there!'

Melanie Brown was so upset she took Sarah away

to the other side of the playground, and sat down on the grass. She felt very miserable.

When they went back into school Miss Bradley saw the other doll.

'Another lovely doll!' she said. 'You two girls will be able to play together at play-time.'

But Melanie Brown and Denise just glared at each other and said nothing.

Later that afternoon, when they were in the hall, Miss Bradley asked Melanie Brown to run back to the classroom and fetch her music book. Melanie Brown loved to be chosen to run errands and she hurried to find the right book so that she could show the children how clever she was, but the first thing she saw when she entered the classroom was the 'walkie-talkie' doll, sitting on Denise's chair. It really was a very pretty doll. Melanie Brown forgot all about the music book and picked up Catherine Elizabeth. She pulled the cord and listened. 'Mama, I'm a good girl – Tell me a story – I like sweeties – I don't want to go to bed – '

Then she walked the doll round the classroom until

she came to her own best doll. Poor Sarah didn't seem exciting any more. Melanie Brown shook the 'walkie-talkie' doll hard.

'It's all your fault, you horrid thing!' she said angrily and she shook it harder. Suddenly there was a funny noise inside the doll's head and Melanie Brown saw that the eyes had gone crooked! Carefully she poked her finger into the eyes to try to straighten them but instead they fell right in! It was terrible. Melanie Brown stared at the doll. She looked ugly without any eyes. Not nearly as pretty as Sarah. Melanie Brown didn't know whether to be glad or sorry. Quickly she sat the doll back on Denise's chair, found the music book, and went into the hall. She wondered what Denise would say when she saw Catherine Elizabeth but it was Jennifer who saw it first.

'Oh, Denise!' she cried. 'Look at your doll! She hasn't got any eyes – she looks horrible!'

Denise took one look and started to cry. Miss Bradley looked round at all the children. They were all staring at the doll except Melanie Brown who was staring at the floor with a very red face.

'How did it happen?' Miss Bradley asked, but Melanie Brown hung her head and wouldn't answer.

'Was it an accident?' she said, but still Melanie Brown said nothing. Miss Bradley sighed.

'You must tell Denise you are sorry,' she said, but Melanie Brown shook her head stubbornly and began to kick the table leg.

'Very well,' said Miss Bradley, 'you must stand out in front of the class in disgrace!'

Melanie Brown was still out in front of the class when it was time to go home, and she began to worry in case she was left there all night!

'I want to go home,' she said in a shaky voice.

'Not until you tell Denise you are sorry,' said Miss Bradley.

Melanie Brown marched up to Denise, who was changing her shoes in the cloakroom.

'SORRY!' she shouted, so loudly that poor Denise nearly jumped out of her skin!

'Not like that!' said Miss Bradley sternly. 'You must say it properly.'

Melanie Brown closed her eyes so that she wouldn't have to see Denise's face.

'I'm sorry,' she said, and although she didn't sound very sorry Miss Bradley thought it would have to do.

By the time Melanie Brown had changed her shoes and put on her coat and hat everyone else had gone home, so she had to walk down the lane on her own.

'Catherine Elizabeth!' she said to herself. 'What a silly name for a doll! Sarah is much nicer. Still, tomorrow I think I'll bring a book.'

Melanie Brown and the Eye-test

Melanie Brown's mother had two pairs of sun-glasses – one pair with blue frames, and one pair with black frames. Melanie Brown had none at all, and she thought it most unfair.

'Why can't *I* have a pair of sun-glasses?' she demanded crossly.

'You don't need any,' said Mrs Brown. 'I get a headache if the sun is very bright, so I wear them to protect my eyes from the glare.'

'I get headaches too,' said Melanie Brown. 'I get one whenever the sun shines. I've got one now.'

'But it's raining now,' said Mrs Brown, hiding a smile behind her hand.

Melanie Brown looked out of the window at the rain. 'Perhaps I need rain-glasses,' she said hopefully, but her mother only laughed. It was very discouraging.

Next morning, however, she had a pleasant surprise. The head-mistress told them that the school nurse was coming to test their eyes.

'My eyes are very good,' said Nicholas, when they were back in the classroom, 'because I eat a lot of carrots. I can see much further than my Dad.'

'I can see for a hundred miles!' said Christopher.

'I can see for two hundred miles!' said Denise, but no one quite believed her. Melanie Brown was just going to say that she could see for three hundred miles with one eye shut, when she had a much better idea. If she could not have any sun-glasses, then perhaps she could have a pair of real glasses.

'I can only see a little bit,' she told them sadly, 'and I get headaches every time it rains.'

They looked at her with interest.

'Every time it rains?' said Nicholas. 'Are you sure?'

'Of course I'm sure,' she said, 'and every time it's sunny.'

They considered this information for a moment.

'What about when it snows?' asked Christopher, at last.

Melanie Brown nodded proudly. 'And when it's foggy, or thundery,' she added.

Denise pointed her finger at Melanie Brown. 'You need glasses,' she said solemnly, and they all agreed. It was most exciting.

'Tell the nurse,' advised Denise, and Melanie Brown promised that she would. She could hardly wait for her turn to have her eyes tested. Nicholas went in first, and was soon back, looking very important.

'It's easy,' he told them. 'You have a piece of cardboard over one of your eyes, and you have to look at letters and pictures and say what they are. I got them all right,' he added proudly.

'I bet Melanie will get them all wrong,' said Christopher gloomily, and they all agreed.

At last her name was called and she went into the hall, followed by the sympathetic glances of her friends. The school nurse smiled at her.

'Hullo, Melanie,' she said. 'I'll just ask you a few questions first. Do you ever get headaches?'

Melanie Brown told her that she did, and she told her about when it rained and snowed, and was thundery or foggy. The nurse listened politely, and then handed her a small piece of cardboard.

'Just hold this over your right eye, dear, and tell me which letter I'm holding up.'

She moved away across the room, and held up the letter 'M'. Melanie Brown screwed up her eyes, and pretended she couldn't see.

' "B" ,' she said.

The nurse held up the letter 'F'.

' "O" ,' said Melanie Brown.

The nurse gave her a long look.

'Don't you know your letters, dear?' she asked, but without waiting for an answer she held up a picture

of an elephant.

'Now dear, can you tell me what this is?'

'A pig,' said Melanie Brown although she knew it was not a pig.

The nurse held up a fish.

'A chicken,' said Melanie Brown, who was beginning to enjoy herself.

'And this one?' said the nurse. It was a shoe.

'A tea-pot,' said Melanie Brown, 'and please may I have my glasses now?'

But the nurse said she didn't have any with her.

'You go back to the classroom,' she said, 'and I'll come and have a word with your teacher.'

Melanie Brown went back to the classroom feeling

very cross. Her friends gathered round her excitedly.

'Where are your glasses?' asked Nicholas, and she had to explain that the nurse didn't have any with her.

'Poor old Melanie!' said Denise. 'Have you still got a headache?'

Melanie Brown nodded. 'It's getting worse!' she said. They all began to comfort her and Christopher gave her a jelly baby to eat at play-time. She began to enjoy herself. Then the nurse came into the room and spoke to Miss Bradley and Miss Bradley called Melanie Brown out to the front. All the children listened eagerly.

'Nurse tells me you couldn't see any of the pictures,' said Miss Bradley. 'Is that so?'

27

Melanie Brown nodded.

'But you always seem to see the blackboard without any trouble,' said Miss Bradley. 'I can't understand it. Are you sure you couldn't see them?'

Melanie Brown nodded again.

'What a shame!' said Miss Bradley. 'Then we shall have to leave you behind when we go to the zoo on Friday because you won't be able to see the animals properly.'

'But I'll have my new glasses!' cried Melanie Brown.

The nurse shook her head.

'I'm afraid they won't be ready by Friday,' she said. 'It takes a long time to make a pair of glasses. Never mind, you will be able to go next year, I expect.'

Melanie Brown stared at her.

'Poor old Melanie!' said Christopher. 'She can't go to the zoo!'

Melanie Brown looked at him and then she looked at Miss Bradley – and then she looked at the nurse.

'It was a joke!' she said firmly. 'I was playing a joke!'

There was a long silence. Everyone waited to see what would happen next.

'A joke!' said Miss Bradley at last. 'Do you call it a joke to waste the nurse's time like that? I certainly don't. I call it naughtiness! You are a very bad girl! You don't deserve to go to the zoo!'

Melanie Brown frowned at her shoes and said nothing. Miss Bradley took her hand.

'You will have to have your eyes tested again,' she said, 'and I will come with you to make sure there's no more nonsense.'

Of course, Melanie Brown managed all the cards that time, so she didn't get a pair of glasses after all. And because she didn't want to miss the visit to the zoo, she tried extra hard to be good for the rest of the day. It was such an effort that by home-time she really did have a headache! Poor Melanie Brown!

Melanie Brown
and Woolly Brown Bear

The children were going to the zoo on Friday, so Miss Bradley talked to them about it on Thursday.

'You will need a packed lunch,' she said, 'a little pocket-money to spend, and a raincoat in case it is wet.'

'Can I bring my doll?' Denise asked, but Miss Bradley shook her head.

'No extras,' she said. 'If you have too many things to think about you are sure to lose something.'

All the children promised to remember but the next morning Melanie Brown marched into school with a teddy bear tucked under her arm.

'Ooh, look!' said Denise indignantly. 'Melanie Brown has brought an extra! It's not fair!'

'He's only small,' said Melanie Brown, smiling her sweetest smile. 'I call him Woolly Brown Bear because that's his name, but sometimes I call him Woolly Brown for short.'

'Well, *I* call him an extra,' said Miss Bradley, 'and you are not going to take him with you to the zoo.'

'Oh, please!' begged Melanie Brown. 'Woolly Brown Bear won't be any trouble, and I won't lose him – I promise! Please let me bring him!'

'No, Melanie,' said Miss Bradley firmly. 'There is

no reason why you should be allowed to bring a toy when none of the other children have brought their toys.'

And she turned away and started to mark the register to make sure that everyone was present who ought to be present.

Now Melanie Brown could be very determined at times. She had made up her mind to take Woolly Brown Bear and she was quite sure she wouldn't enjoy the zoo a bit without him. So when no one was looking she opened her satchel and stuffed him in on top of her sandwiches. When her name was called out she answered brightly and Miss Bradley was pleasantly surprised to see that she was not sulking. But of course she didn't know about Woolly Brown Bear!

'Right!' said Miss Bradley at last. 'Now it's time to go!'

The coach ride was great fun. Melanie Brown sat on the back seat with all her friends. There was so much to see and talk about she almost wished it could last for ever, but in no time at all they were at the zoo, and Miss Bradley was telling them not to wander too far in case they got lost.

The children had never seen so many animals. They saw tiny grey monkeys and large grey elephants; dainty gazelles and clumsy hippos; noisy parrots and silent snakes. They heard the lions roar and they laughed at the penguins and they watched the sealions being fed. Before they knew it the morning had slipped away and it was time to rest and eat their lunch. Thankfully they sat down under a big shady

tree and opened up their satchels. Melanie Brown
had forgotten all about Woolly Brown Bear but the
moment she opened her satchel he fell out on to the
grass in front of everyone. Miss Bradley could hardly
believe her eyes.

'Melanie Brown!' she cried. 'You really are the
limit! Fancy bringing that bear with you after all I've
said!'

But she didn't want to spoil the day with a grumble,
so she said no more, but Melanie Brown knew what
she was thinking and she went very red. Quickly she
pushed Woolly Brown Bear down among the big roots
of the tree and hoped Miss Bradley would forget about
him. Then she turned her attention to her lunch,
which was delicious. There were sausage rolls and egg
sandwiches, an apple and a banana. There was a fizzy

drink, too, which Miss Bradley opened for her with a special tin opener. By the time she had finished she was very full and felt rather sleepy, but Miss Bradley said they would have to look lively if they wanted to see everything before they went home.

The giraffes were much taller than Melanie Brown had imagined, and the buffaloes were much hairier. The camels were humpier, the chimpanzees were funnier, the . . . zebras . . . were . . . stripier . . . Melanie Brown was so tired her legs would hardly carry her along. Even Miss Bradley was weary.

'We'll just see the bears,' she said, 'and then we'll go back to the coach, and – what's the matter, Christopher?'

'It's Melanie – she's crying,' said Christopher. Melanie Brown lifted a tear-stained face.

'I've lost W-Woolly Brown B-Bear,' she sobbed. For once in her life Miss Bradley was speechless – but Denise wasn't!

'Serves you right!' she said. 'You shouldn't have brought him!'

'Denise is right,' sighed Miss Bradley, 'but that doesn't alter the fact that he's lost. Can you remember where you had him last?'

'I can!' said Nicholas. 'It was under that tree where we had our sandwiches.'

Then, of course, Melanie Brown remembered pushing him down into the big roots.

'Well,' said Miss Bradley, 'we certainly can't go back for him now. It would take too long and the driver won't wait. I'll phone the zoo tomorrow,

Melanie, and ask about him. Someone will find him, I'm sure. So stop crying and we'll go and see the real bears!'

But Melanie Brown's day was quite spoiled. She trailed along behind the others and hardly glanced at the big black bears or the tiny koalas. She was so tired and miserable that she fell asleep on the way home. But even asleep she could not forget her troubles. She dreamed of poor Woolly Brown Bear lying all alone under the cold night sky!

Next day, however, Miss Bradley phoned the zoo and the keeper soon found him. He made Woolly Brown Bear into a parcel with brown paper and string and posted him back to the school. Melanie Brown was *so* pleased to see him again she gave him a great big hug which nearly squashed him flat!

Melanie Brown's Exciting News

Ten o'clock in the morning was news-time. The children tidied away the paints and bricks and crayons and closed the door on the Wendy House. Then they sat in a little group with Miss Bradley to tell each other their news. Melanie Brown loved news-time when she had some news to tell, but she didn't much care for listening to other people's news. She soon got very bored.

'My Auntie's coming to stay,' Nicholas told them one morning, 'and she's going to stay the night – and she's got a baby – and I'm going to sleep in the – '

'People are *always* coming to stay with us!' said Melanie Brown, interrupting him, but Miss Bradley frowned at her and said, 'Go on Nicholas.'

But Melanie Brown's interruption had made him forget what he was going to say. He stared hopefully at the ceiling but it didn't help, so Miss Bradley said he could have another turn later if he remembered.

Then it was Susan's turn.

'I'm getting a pencil case for my birthday,' she said, 'and it's going to be a wooden one, with a lid that slides!'

She sat down again and Melanie Brown leaned across to Christopher.

'I've already got one,' she said, 'and they're no good because the lid keeps getting stuck!'

But Christopher wasn't listening. He was waving his arm furiously to catch Miss Bradley's eye.

'We'd better hear Christopher's news,' she laughed, 'before he goes off bang!'

He jumped to his feet.

'My Dad's building a garage,' he said proudly, 'and it's going to be bricks and concrete – and my Mum says he's not to walk it all into the kitchen or she'll be mad!'

While Miss Bradley was saying how clever Christopher's father was, Melanie Brown was racking her brains to try and think of some news. The trouble was nothing exciting was happening at her house just then. At last she could bear it no longer, and she put up her hand.

'Melanie?'

She stood up slowly and then stared Miss Bradley straight in the eye.

'We're going on holiday,' she said, ' – to Africa!'

There was an amazed silence.

'And when we come back my Auntie's coming to stay – and she's got hundreds of babies! – And my Mummy's got a necklace made of real diamonds! – And it's my birthday today!'

She sat down amid cries of astonishment and disbelief. Her eyes gleamed triumphantly as she looked round at the other children and then she looked at Miss Bradley. Miss Bradley seemed to be having a coughing fit, and was hiding her face in her handkerchief. Or was she laughing? Melanie Brown looked at her suspiciously. Denise put her hand up and Miss Bradley nodded to her.

'It can't be her birthday,' said Denise, 'because hers is after mine and I haven't had mine yet!'

Melanie Brown scowled but then Christopher spoke up.

'How can she be going to Africa?' he asked. 'They're coming on holiday with us, and we're going to Butlins!'

Melanie Brown began to explain that the Butlins they were going to was *in* Africa but Miss Bradley shook her head.

'Melanie was just having a game with us,' she said. 'But it certainly was exciting! But now *I* have some news for you.'

The children stared at her open-mouthed. A teacher having news? Whatever next!

'I am going to be married soon,' she told them. 'I shall still be your teacher but I shall have a new name. I shall be Mrs Collins.'

'What a funny name!' said Susan.

'I don't think it's funny,' said Melanie Brown quickly and then she added, 'Do you need any bridesmaids?'

Miss Bradley said that she didn't.

'Can I be a page-boy, then?' Melanie Brown asked hopefully, but Christopher said only boys could be page-boys. It was very disappointing.

That afternoon they had great fun, making a big fluffy sheep out of tissue paper. Melanie Brown forgot her disappointment and stuck on tissue paper as fast as she could. But then Miss Bradley said she needed someone to paint the sheep's nose and feet black.

'Me! Me!' cried everyone, but Miss Bradley could only choose one and she chose John. Then Melanie Brown lost interest in the tissue paper and went into the book corner to be miserable. She was waiting for Miss Bradley to notice her but Miss Bradley was too busy. When the sheep was finished it looked quite real and they were all very pleased with their handiwork. They cleared away the scraps of tissue paper and Miss Bradley washed the paste brushes. Melanie Brown was still sitting in the book corner and at last Miss Bradley noticed her.

'Oh, that's where you're hiding is it?' she said 'Come out and look at our sheep. I think it needs some grass to eat. Perhaps tomorrow you could draw some with a green felt-tipped pen.'

Melanie Brown cheered up at once and came out of the book corner to admire the sheep. The rest of the class were getting their hats and coats on because it was home-time. Miss Bradley looked down at Melanie Brown's hands.

'Goodness!' she said. 'Look how sticky you are! You had better wash your hands before you go home.'

The other children said 'goodbye' and hurried out. Melanie Brown didn't like being last so she rushed for the soap. Just as she took it in her hand she noticed something sparkling deep down in the plug hole of the sink.

'Miss Bradley!' she cried. 'Come quickly and see what this is!'

Miss Bradley took one look and gasped. She looked at her hand and saw that her engagement ring was missing.

'Good gracious!' she said. 'That's my ring down there! Oh, you are a clever girl to have seen it! It must have come off while I was washing the brushes! I must ask Mr Bloggs to get it up for me. He'll be here in a minute.'

When Mr Bloggs arrived he unscrewed the pipe and got the ring out. Miss Bradley was so pleased that she gave him some money to buy some tobacco. And she gave Melanie Brown six toffees from her special tin!

'And tomorrow,' said Melanie Brown triumphantly, 'I really will have something exciting to tell at news-time!'

And she was right!

Melanie Brown is Too Helpful

The school television set was not at all like the set in Melanie Brown's home. It was much bigger and stood on four legs, at one end of the hall. There were two doors at the front which were always kept locked until the teachers opened them with a small key. When it was time to watch the television the children all carried chairs into the hall and arranged them in rows.

Melanie Brown looked forward to the television programmes. One was about puppets and the other was about fire-engines and shops and animals and aeroplanes – and so many things there is no time to tell them all! As soon as they went into the hall Miss Bradley would switch the set on at the wall, and while it was warming up she would pull the curtains to shut out the light.

Now one day Melanie Brown was feeling helpful. She had given out the milk without spilling a single drop. She had found a missing piece of jigsaw, and she had cleaned the blackboard. She was still feeling particularly helpful when they went into the hall to watch the puppets. To her surprise Miss Bradley went straight over to the windows to pull the curtains, so Melanie Brown guessed at once that she had forgotten to switch the set on and without a moment's hesitation she ran across to the wall and flicked the switch! She was very pleased with herself. Four helpful things in one morning! She sat down on her chair feeling very proud and they all waited for the programme to begin.

They waited and waited – and waited! But nothing happened.

'That's funny,' said Miss Bradley. 'I wonder what's wrong. It was working before play-time. I'll have a look at it.'

She looked at the back of the set to see if the aerial was properly connected, because sometimes it worked loose. Not this time, though. She twiddled all the knobs and tried the other channels. Nothing. She looked up at the clock and frowned.

'Oh dear! We have missed the beginning.' she said. 'I had better tell Miss Grainger. Just sit quietly for a moment, children.'

Miss Grainger was the head-mistress, so they all knew it was a serious matter. They sat like mice until Miss Bradley and Miss Grainger came into the hall. Miss Grainger did all the things that Miss Bradley had done but still the television remained quite blank.

'How very odd,' said Miss Grainger. 'You say it was working perfectly before play?'

'Yes,' said Miss Bradley. 'Mrs Jones's class watched something and she left it on for us.'

'I'll give Mr Bloggs a ring,' said Miss Grainger. 'It will only take a minute or two to have a look at it. And what nice patient children you are!' she said, turning to them. 'I think Melanie Brown is one of the quietest.'

Melanie Brown beamed with delight and Miss Bradley smiled at her. Soon Mr Bloggs arrived on his bicycle with a book of instructions in his pocket. He marched into the hall and opened the book importantly. Then he glared at Miss Bradley.

'Can't we have a bit more light in here?' he asked sternly, and Miss Bradley hurried to draw back the curtains. He turned over several pages and said 'Aha!' and scratched his nose. Melanie Brown thought it was almost as much fun watching Mr Bloggs as it would have been watching the puppets!

'I think it's your power pack,' he said at last and retired behind the set. They could see his feet and legs and they could hear him breathing heavily. Then he said 'Damn!' in a loud voice.

Melanie Brown was shocked.

'He said "Damn",' she said. 'He shouldn't say that!'

'Poor Mr Bloggs,' said Miss Bradley. 'I'm sure he didn't mean it. I think he's hurt himself.'

Mr Bloggs reappeared, looking hot and flustered.

'Can't have been off long,' he grumbled. 'It's still hot!'

He looked hopefully at the screen, which remained empty.

'Why don't you thump it?' cried Christopher. 'That's what my Dad does!'

Mr Bloggs raised his hand and for one thrilling moment they thought he was going to, but he hesitated.

'Better not,' he said reluctantly, dropping his hand. He had another look in his book, then shook his head.

'Could it be something wrong with the aerial itself?' suggested Miss Bradley.

'Ah, that'll be it!' he said. 'I reckon you've hit the nail on the head! The aerial! Now that'll be a job for the aerial people, not me! I'll tell Miss Grainger to get in touch with them right away.'

They watched him go regretfully.

'Now we can't see the puppets,' wailed Denise.

'Never mind,' said Miss Bradley. 'I expect it will be mended in time for tomorrow's programme. Now, take your chairs back to the classroom. I'll just switch off the – '

She stopped in the middle of the sentence and stared at the switch. 'It's not switched on! But Mrs Jones said it was!'

She put the switch down and waited, watching the set. Music and pictures appeared and all the children clapped their hands and cheered. But Miss Bradley didn't cheer. She switched it off again and looked round. The children took one look at her face and stopped cheering.

'Did anyone touch this switch?' she asked quietly.

Melanie Brown put her hand up and Miss Bradley groaned.

'Not you again, Melanie?' she said faintly.

'I only switched it on,' said Melanie Brown, 'because you forgot.'

'I did *not* forget!' said Miss Bradley. 'I didn't need to switch it on because it was already on! You must have switched it off!'

There was a terrible silence.

'Oh well, I suppose you didn't mean it,' said Miss Bradley. 'But I don't think Miss Grainger's going to be too pleased about it.'

Melanie Brown thought it was very ungrateful of Miss Bradley to talk like that and decided not to help her ever again. She told Miss Bradley what she had decided and Miss Bradley said, 'Is that a threat or a promise!'

Sometimes, thought Melanie Brown, teachers could be very difficult!

Melanie Brown and the Big Ball

Sometimes when the weather was fine, the children went into the playground with three big wire baskets. These baskets were full of exciting things. There were little square bags called bean-bags which the children threw to each other. Sometimes they balanced them on their heads or jumped around with the bean-bag held between their feet. That was really quite difficult.

There were bats, too, small cricket bats and ping-pong bats, and plenty of balls, all colours and sizes. There were skipping ropes, as well, and bamboo canes to jump over.

Melanie Brown liked the big balls best. One day, when the sun was shining, they carried the wire baskets into the playground and Melanie Brown chose a big blue ball.

'Now remember,' said Miss Bradley, 'don't throw the balls too high or too far because they might go over the fence into the lane. Try to be sensible with them.'

Melanie Brown *did* try, and she *was* sensible. She threw the big ball up a little way and caught it. She did that five times! Miss Bradley said, 'Clever girl,' because, after all, she was only five years old.

Then they changed over and tried something else.

Melanie Brown got a skipping rope out of the basket, but though she tried very hard she could not skip. It was very annoying, because Melanie liked to be good at everything. She kept trying, but it was no good. She felt cross with herself and cross with the rope, so she threw it back into the wire basket.

She took the blue ball out of the basket again, and she was so pleased to be doing something she was good at, that she threw the ball very, very high. She was quite sure she could catch it. She watched it go up and up and held out her arms for it. But it did not come down again!

The school roof was quite flat, and that is where the ball landed. Right on the edge of the roof, nearly in the gutter. Melanie Brown stared up, open-mouthed. She could just see a little bit of blue. She looked round hastily to see if Miss Bradley had noticed, but she was watching Christopher. Melanie Brown picked up the skipping-rope again and tried to skip.

'Good, Melanie,' said Miss Bradley. 'I think you'll be able to skip before long if you keep on trying.'

She cheered up at once, and began to practise and once the rope did come up over her head properly, and once or twice it went under her feet properly, and soon she forgot all about the big blue ball.

After dinner all the children went out to play and Mrs Jones went out with them to make sure no one was rough, and to look after anyone who fell over.

All the big children were out in the playground as well as Melanie Brown's class. Some of the big children were nearly eleven. Melanie Brown sat on the grass and watched two of the big boys wrestling. They rolled about on the grass, pulling and pushing and yelling at the top of their voices, and then sat up laughing, red in the face. Melanie Brown thought it was a silly game. Suddenly, one of the boys glanced up at the roof, and he saw the big blue ball.

'Mrs Jones, Mrs Jones,' he cried, 'there's a ball on the roof!'

Everyone stared up at the roof. Melanie Brown

stared too. Mrs Jones walked across the playground to get a better view.

'So there is,' she said. 'I wonder how that got up there.'

The boy who had first seen the ball got very excited.

'Please can I get it down, Mrs Jones? I saw it first.'

'Well, someone will have to get it down,' she said. 'But I don't think you can reach it.'

'Please, Mrs Jones, there's a broom round by the shed – the gardener's broom. I could knock it down with that.'

And he rushed away round the corner of the school and was soon back with the broom. He held it by its bristly end and stretched up as high as he could but the end of the handle did not quite reach the ball. So Mrs Jones told him to take the broom back again.

Then one of the big girls had an idea.

'Mrs Jones, I think there's a ladder in the shed, because Mr Bloggs had one when the gutter was overflowing.'

Mrs Jones sent her into school to ask the headmistress for the key to the shed. There *was* a ladder in there and it was just long enough to reach the gutter. So a boy went up the ladder, while Mrs Jones held it steady.

Melanie Brown held her breath as the boy reached the gutter and picked up the big blue ball. He could not hold the ball while he climbed down, so he threw it down into the playground.

And a very odd thing happened. The ball bounced on the ground and then bounced up and hit Melanie

Brown in the tummy! She fell over backwards, and sat there on the ground staring at the ball. It was just as though the ball knew that she had thrown it up there and was punishing her!

All the children laughed, but one of the big girls helped her up again and brushed her skirt down.

When the ladder was put back in the shed again, Mrs Jones came over to her.

'Poor Melanie,' she said. 'That was bad luck, wasn't it? Never mind, you're not hurt, are you?'

Melanie Brown shook her head slowly. She did not answer because she was thinking. Next time they took out the wire baskets she would leave the balls well alone and learn to skip!

Melanie Brown's Birthday Party

Melanie Brown could be very awkward at times and one of the times was when she was planning her birthday party.

'I want everyone in the whole school to come,' she told her mother hopefully.

'Don't be silly, dear,' said Mrs Brown.

'Well, the whole class, then.'

'No, Melanie!' said her mother patiently. 'You know we couldn't possibly fit all those children in. Do be sensible.'

Melanie Brown thought about it.

'Well then,' she said, 'I want Mr Bloggs to come because he rescued me when I was up the tree, and I want the milkman to come – '

'If you don't stop being silly,' said Mrs Brown, 'no one will come because you won't have a party! Just think of five of your friends.'

So Melanie Brown decided to ask Christopher, Denise, Paula, Nicholas and John. Mrs Brown bought a packet of invitation cards and they sent one each to the five children and they all said they could come. Mrs Brown made a birthday cake with 'MELANIE' on it in pink icing, and bought some pink slippers to match Melanie Brown's best pink dress. Melanie

Brown was so excited that she counted the days to the party! But then – oh dear! She quarrelled with her five friends! This is how it happened.

It was play-time and the six children were playing together on the grass.

'We'll play witches,' said Melanie Brown, 'and that bush can be the witch's house and you are all walking past – '

'It could be a gingerbread house!' said Paula. 'Like the one in *Hansel and Gretel*.'

'All right, then, a gingerbread house,' said Melanie Brown, 'and you are all walking past – '

'And we all eat the house!' cried Nicholas and he began to make loud eating noises. Melanie Brown frowned at him severely.

'Don't keep interrupting,' she said. 'I have to say what we do because it's my game.'

'It's not your game!' said Paula.

'It is!' cried Melanie Brown. 'I thought of it!'

'But I thought of the gingerbread house – '

'It doesn't matter whose game it is,' said John. 'Let's get on with it. Who's going to be the witch?'

'I am!' cried the three girls together.

John laughed. 'We can't have three witches!' he said.

'I should be the witch,' said Melanie Brown, 'because I'm the oldest.'

'You're not!' said Christopher. 'I'm the oldest.'

'Oh,' said Melanie Brown, 'then I should be the witch because I'm the youngest!'

'You're not the youngest,' said Denise.

Then they began to argue and Melanie Brown got crosser and crosser.

'If you don't let me be the witch then I won't let you come to my party!' she shouted.

'Don't want to come to your silly old party!' said Denise. 'So there!'

Melanie Brown was so shocked she hardly knew what to say.

'You're all horrible!' she said, nearly bursting into tears. 'I hate you and you're not coming to my party!'

And she ran away to find a corner to cry in.

But none of the children told their mothers about the quarrel – not even Melanie Brown. Instead she found the packet of invitation cards and filled in the seven cards that were left with different names. Next

day she gave them out to the seven children and they took them home to show their mothers. While all this was happening Mrs Brown was busy buying things for the party. She bought six crackers and six funny hats and she made six jellies. By the time Friday came round Melanie Brown had got over her temper and she told her five best friends that they *could* come after all! So altogether she had invited twelve children but Mrs Brown didn't know that!

Saturday afternoon came at last and Melanie Brown put on her pink dress and the pink slippers and felt very fine. Paula arrived and then John, quickly followed by Christopher, Nicholas and Denise. They each gave her a present and she was busily unwrapping them when the door bell rang again.

'I'll see who it is,' said Grandmother, who had also come to the party. Jennifer stood on the step with her mother.

'I do hope we're not too early,' said Jennifer's mother.

Grandmother shook her head and led Jennifer into the lounge to join the others. Mrs Brown looked rather puzzled but before she could say anything the bell

53

rang again! This time Mr Brown went to answer it while Mrs Brown and Grandmother stared at each other in dismay.

When all twelve children had arrived the three grown-ups left them opening presents and rushed into the kitchen to wonder what to do!

'Isn't it awful!' wailed Mrs Brown. 'All those children! We haven't enough chairs – or plates – or funny hats. Everything will be spoiled! I just can't understand how it's happened.'

It was a good thing Grandmother was there because she was very wise. She sorted things out in no time. Father went to the nearest shop for some cardboard cups and plates. Mother took the children into the garden for some party games and Grandmother made some more sandwiches. The six jellies went into the fridge for another day and the crackers and funny hats went into the cupboard to wait for Christmas.

Tea was a picnic in the garden and everyone agreed it was much more fun than an ordinary tea. After tea they played some more games until it was time to go home.

When Mrs Brown tucked Melanie Brown into bed that night she asked her how it was that so many children came to the party, and Melanie Brown told her.

'But it was so much fun!' she said. 'Can I ask them all again next year?'

Mrs Brown laughed. 'I'll think about it,' she said.

An Argentine Tango

Produced by:

FriesenPress

Suite 300 – 852 Fort Street
Victoria, BC, Canada V8W 1H8

www.friesenpress.com

Distributed to the trade by The Ingram Book Company

An Argentine Tango

A Narrative Description of the Dance

Harry Lindwall

1 *A Narrative Description of the Dance*

THE DANCE

He watched as the couples gathered on the dance floor, waiting for the music to begin. Then he stood up, just slightly before she did, and both walked to the dance floor. They faced each other, and she slipped her right hand into his upright palm, stepped toward him into a close embrace, and rested her arm softly on his shoulder. He enclosed her waist with his forearm, then moved it up to allow his fingers to loosely curve around her side. He felt the sloping curve of her back: smooth and exciting through the silken dress.

When the music started he thought, *good*! It was an old tango with a sharp, steady beat and lulls that hovered, and offered places for him to dwell with his feelings.

3   *A Narrative Description of the Dance*

He started gently-almost imperceptibly-to shift his weight from foot to foot; she sensed it through the closeness of their bodies and began to follow. At the beginning of a phrase of music he stepped sharply back on his right foot, moving his body with it, then took a long, smooth step to the side with his left foot. She felt the movements of his body through the embrace and followed them, their feet hitting the floor together on each beat.

He paused and tightened the embrace with his forearm as she stood balanced over her right leg; he now began to slowly rotate their upper bodies together in smooth, shallow arcs from side to side. Each reversal, marked by a beat of the music, kindled their feeling of a connection to each other and to the music. As she pivoted, her left leg was folded backward at the knee, and he saw the slim shape of her lower leg and the red and gold high-heeled shoe. An image from a film flashed through his head: the films' star, standing in that way, as she was being passionately kissed.

He stopped, and faced down the line of dance, waiting as the music in his head flowed into his

5   *A Narrative Description of the Dance*

emotions. Then he lifted his right foot, crossed it over his left and led three quick forward steps. She followed, but on the last step, she smoothly lifted her left heel and gracefully crossed it tightly to the right of her right foot, then immediately balanced on it. As he watched, he thought, *She performs the cruzada with a beautiful, feminine style of her own.*

He stood quietly, tightening the embrace, feeling the contours of her body against him; then he moved his body forward, leading her to step her right foot back. He now moved his left foot - not forward, but to be in back of her left leg. As the caves of their legs met, she lifted hers' up, then folded it back at the knee, and he sharply rotated her upper body to the left on a beat of music, and she performed a high, sweeping *boleo*, balanced on her right leg. He supported her balance; then waited as he passed the lead to her, and the tempo of the dance slowed. She seemed to hang there; then with deliberate, goddess- like movements she brought the inside of her left foot to her right leg and slowly slid it up the leg to her knee then crossed it over to the right side,and then down her leg to come

7 *A Narrative Description of the Dance*

to rest in a *cruzada* as she rotated seductively back to face him. He had a thirst for it when he felt her slender, soft fingers on his neck as he closed their embrace and finished the *salida*.

He was deeply into it now. Even as his mind stayed clear and focused, the feelings from the closeness of their movements and the insistent, deliberateness of the music were flooding through him. He thought of the movements he wanted to lead her through and the patterns he wanted them to do together, but he knew for it to feel true to him afterward - for him to have that deep, quiet feeling inside - he knew that he must dance his own tango. There could be no choreography; he would dance only the elements that appealed to him, the ones he had learned well, because he took pleasure doing them. He would connect these to the music and to his mood at each moment; there would be pauses for them to feel the emotions, and for her to express herself with flourishes of staccato steps. Then it would be *his* tango.

He knew that he could lead tango well, because from the beginning he had always kept in his mental awareness the position of his partners

9 A Narrative Description of the Dance

legs and feet (just as when driving his car the periphery of the car is modeled into his mind as if it were a part of his own body). He had learned to always know the position of her standing foot, to feel its anchor point through her embrace, and to verify it by pivoting her: sensing it through her upper body. This allowed him to move his body close to her standing foot and to then be able to move her gracefully in any direction.

Sometimes, as he did now, he lifted her slightly with his right arm, signaling her to stay on that foot as he moved around her, and she pivoted on it, and he controlled the angle of her leaning body by balancing their upper bodies against each other. Their reliance on, and trust in, each other increased as he moved further and further away, circling and lowering the angle of her body. Then he stopped and waited, not wanting to let go of the feeling of closeness between them. When the music changed, he stepped toward her, closing the distance between them until she was upright, then he relaxed his right arm and both moved together down the line of dance.

11 *A Narrative Description of the Dance*

Each step became a subtle composition as they walked together, locked in a close embrace. Their toes were turned partially outwould to give them balance, and he began each step by moving his body forward. She responded by immediately projecting her foot backward. He carefully proportioned the time between his forward stride and the collection of his trailing foot by dividing the interval between the beats of music to fit his feeling of what he wanted his cadence to be. He then measured the length of each of his steps by the extension of his knee, and she lowered her foot to the floor on a beat of music each time she felt the slowing of his body's forword movement.

Both dancers showed that they had a sense of their appearance, and their style, and to the smoothness of their movements as they danced, but now each had become aware mostly of what they were feeling and were unaware that their emotions were being manifested in both the movements of their bodies and in the intentions that they projected toward each other.

He now began to feel something he was always looking for: the sense of a deepening

13 *A Narrative Description of the Dance*

connection between him and his partner. They were no longer two dancers- they had melded together on both a physical and mental level, freely feeling and enjoying the excitement of their movements and their contact with each other. He didn't know why he always searched for and needed this feeling of connection as much as he did, but he did know it was the reason he continued to dance tango and why he kept coming back to dance it again and again.

He began another *salida,* and as he stepped to his left and led her in two smooth back *ochos,* he quickly moved his right foot next to her trailing foot, signaling her to stop. His movements then became slow and gentle as he lifted her right foot slightly with the tip of his shoe, and guided it clockwise. She rotated on her standing foot, complying with a uniquely feminine acceptance. Now, he quickly moved his left foot to the other side of her foot, straddling it. Then he stepped back with his right foot and, as their eyes met, it became an invitation to her to step forward across their connected feet. Their eyes stayed locked as she performed a low, wide, sweeping *boleo;* she then returned her foot

to his again with a series of rhythmic tapping steps and a seductive touch of his leg as she stepped over. He felt a familiar tightness in his throat as he received her affirmation. She continued with a sidestep around him as he rotated his body clockwise; then he projected his right leg through her legs ,and moved forward onto it, pivoting both their bodies as she raised her trailing leg up over his, and rotated onto a back step.

He again took her into a close embrace as they both stood on their right legs. He stepped forward with his left foot and led her to step back onto her left foot, then he pivoted her body a quarter of a turn to his right and led her to take another back step as he moved his right foot to the side. For the first few steps, he had to force himself to stay focused to be able to repeat the pattern every two beats of music, but then as he steered it at an angle down the line of dance, it began to feel rhythmic and nicely elegant

He realized suddenly, that the music was coming to an end, and he began listening, waiting to hear the familiar musical ending

sequence. He paused as they faced each other, then took a forward step with his left foot and rocked back onto his right. She followed, and he took her into a tight embrace with his right arm and began a long step backward with his left leg, bringing her with him as he bent his right knee and slowly lowered both their bodies down toward the floor. Their eyes stayed fixed, staring into each others' face, as their trailing legs stretched out along the floor while the last notes sounded.

After a few moments, they rose and smiled at each other, feeling slightly embarrassed, as if they had just realized where they were.

He did not know this woman; he did not even know if he would get to know her, or ever dance with her again, or if they would perhaps, become friends, or lovers. He did know that there had been a connection between them, and that it had lasted no more then three minutes, but it had been a connection in which they had shared a freedom to merge together and, with the music, to express their personal and sub-conscious feelings with their bodies.

19 *A Narrative Description of the Dance*

THE THOUGHTS

Later at home, lying on his bed, thoughts of the *milonga* flowed through his head; as they often did. It had been a good night of tango! There had been many partners; some had been good dancers, some not so good, but many had shown a desire to express themselves and to be led by his movements. He had felt their excitement and it had heightened his own and they were able together, to share good tango.

Now other, different thoughts came that he had to pay attention to. Was he being seduced by tango? Was he spending too much of his time, energy and emotion on it? He knew others who had spent themselves on it, ignoring careers and personal interests.

Some had used it only to search for romance, but these usually proved to be no more stable than romance found off the dance floor. *Even so, the allure is very strong,* he thought; *the gracefully moving, perfumed partners and always the pull of passion between you.* He had been in love, and it had been like a heady drug, but in the end it held deep pain and the assurance that you can not really completely know another person.

Then was it just an enjoyable waste of time; a way to spend yourself before you die? For him, there was something more. It was those moments when both he and his partner were not themselves. When they became something new, something created out of movement and music and their own feelings. It was these moments that satisfied, soothed, and changed something inside him and this was good.

No, he thought: *tango could not be his whole life, but it is a vital and sweet part of it.*

23 *A Narrative Description of the Dance*

THE CONCEPTS

The leader creates a dance for the follower to perform. He uses the movements of his body to lead her as he takes the music inside himself; then shares it with her through his movements.

The leader must always try to present the follower so she experiences herself as the centerpiece of - and a beautiful complement to - the dance.

The follower abandons herself and connects to the leaders movements by sharing a close and intimate embrace. Within the embrace each partner keeps their own balance and takes great care not to disturb the balance of the other.

The basic steps of the follower are simple and clear: she is led forward or back or to either

side. She never takes a step or changes which foot her weight is on, unless led to do so by the leader. If the leader rotates his body, she performs a simple but rigidly-set pattern of forward step, side step, back step, side step, around him. These steps can be started or stopped at any place in the sequence by the leader. Most of the followers steps require her to pivot as she performs them; her mastery of this simple but elegent movement greatly affects the appearance and efficacy of her dance. The follower can also be led to perform a *cruzada* in which she steps back with her right foot, slides her left foot next to it on the right side, and transfers her weight on to it. A beautiful and elegant tango can be danced with just these simple basic steps. Other more challenging elements the follower might want to performare are highly stylized, and are studied and practiced by the leader and follower together to experience and develop the mastery of their bodies movements to the music.

There is no "book of rules" for the performance of a social Argentine tango, and many styles have evolved along with new music. New steps

27 *A Narrative Description of the Dance*

and patterns are often developed by the dancers and are either accepted or rejected by other dancers worldwide.

The dance can be expressive of the personal feelings of the dancers to many things, but most often it is to each other and to the music. It can be danced deliberately languid or flashingly fast according to the preference and mood of the dancers and the music selected. The music is some of the most beautiful in the world and ranges from the emotional excitement of a single *bandoneon* to a philharmonic composition.

The dance is performed in almost every country, with each contributing their own discrete touches of individuality, yet all can be recognized as an Argentine tango - a stylized dance of expression and connection and shared emotions.

This book is dedicated to
two talented and passionate tango instructors
Mariel Gonzales
&
Richard Lucia

Lightning Source UK Ltd.
Milton Keynes UK
UKOW02f1759300115

245431UK00001B/16/P